OLiViA'S Secret Scribbles

My (Almost) Perfect Puppy

Kane Miller
A DIVISION OF EDC PUBLISHING

For Mo Johnson and Fat Beagle, and our
(almost) perfect puppies, Benji and Pip—M.C.

For Zoe, Jade and our own crazy pooch, Marley—D.M.

First American Edition 2019
Kane Miller, A Division of EDC Publishing

Text copyright © Meredith Costain, 2018
Illustrations copyright © Danielle McDonald, 2018

First published by Scholastic Australia Pty Limited in 2018.
This edition published under license from Scholastic Australia Pty Limited.

For information contact:
Kane Miller, A Division of EDC Publishing
5402 S 122nd E Ave
Tulsa, OK 74146
www.kanemiller.com
www.myubam.com

Library of Congress Control Number: 2018942396

Printed and bound in the United States of America

5 6 7 8 9 10 11 12 13 14

ISBN: 978-1-61067-840-7

OLiViA'S
BiG BOOK of
PRiVate
SECRETS
DO NOT OPEN!
GO AWAY!

KEEP OUT

KEEP OUT

(This means you, Max,
and mainly you, Ella!!!)

Star-moves Monday

Matilda and I were **roller-weaving** in my driveway today.

"Roller-weaving"

Roller—weaving is a game we invented. You have to weave around **soccer cones,** just like you do when you're dribbling a ball at soccer practice. Except you don't need a ball. And you do it on **roller skates!**

Matilda is my new best friend. Her family moved into the house behind ours a few weeks ago. When we want to visit each other, we just climb through a hole in the back fence! ☺

Matilda's HOUSE

OUR house

FENCE

Matilda and I are both *STAR* roller-weavers. Here are some of the moves we can do:

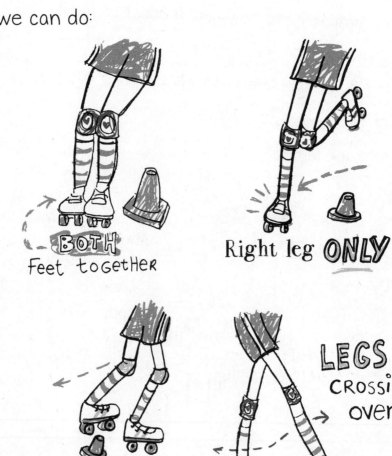

BOTH
Feet togeteR

Right leg ONLY

Backward

LEGS CROSSING over

We were just trying out a **really tricky** new move when Bob ran over and stole one of the soccer cones. Then he **ran off** around the backyard with it!

We had to stop our game and get the cone back before he chewed it up into **teeny tiny little pieces!** 😳

Bob is very friendly and cuddly. But he can also get into **trouble** sometimes! (Just like me. ☺)

BOB♥

He's always sneaking up
onto the couch when
we're watching TV,
even though he's
not allowed to.

NO DOGS allowed

Or even when we're not watching TV.

I invented some special Anti-Lying-On-The-Couch itching POWDER to stop him doing it.

BAKING SODA

Anti-Lying-ON-THE-COUCH itching POWDER

FLOUR

COCOA

TALCUM PoWDER

But it didn't work.

Bob still gets up on the couch. Especially when he thinks we're not looking. ☹

He also loves digging holes in the backyard. He buries stuff out there for us to find later. He thinks it's a really good game!

Things Bob buries in our backyard

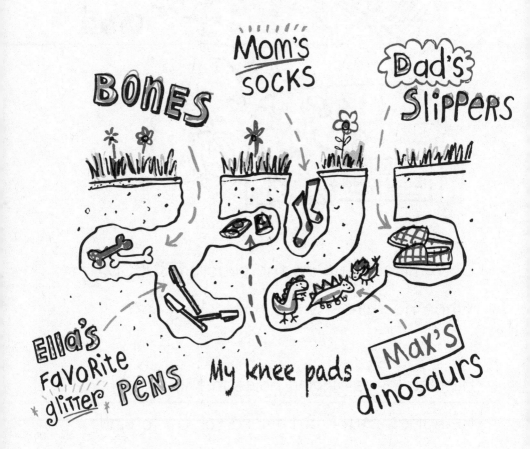

Bob also loves **chasing** Donkey. He thinks that's a **really good game** too!

Donkey doesn't. ☹

Donkey belongs to our next-door neighbor. He loves to lie in the sun on the roof outside my bedroom.

He's a big **grumpy pants**, but also very smart. I'm training him to be a **super-duper detective cat!**

But most of all, Bob loves **eating!**

He eats everything. Even broccoli. (Yuck.)

And he loves raiding the trash can in the middle of the night. This morning we found trash all over the kitchen floor.

I think Bob was hoping we'd blame it on
Donkey. But we know who it **really was.**
Dad took this photo to prove it. Hehehe. ☺

So today, Mom put the trash can inside
our pantry where it will be safe from Bob.
I don't think he's very happy about that.

☺livia

Trouble Tuesday

BOB is in BIG trouble.

Last night, while we were all asleep, he sneaked into the pantry and raided the trash can AGAIN! This morning, there were scraps of food and bits of trash all over the floor. And also in his tummy.

Mom says Bob will get sick if he keeps eating the trash. So I am making a new invention called a Pantry Trash Protector. It will let us know if Bob tries to sneak into the pantry again.

Here are my plans for it.

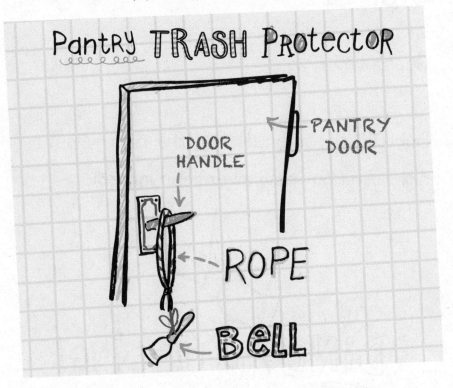

I am going to test out my new invention
tonight!

☺livia

Bigger Trouble Wednesday

Guess what?

Bob **did** try to sneak into the pantry last night. And my new invention worked!

DING! Ding! DING!

As soon as I heard the bell I jumped out of bed and ran downstairs to the kitchen. Mom was already there.

Bob was lying down with his nose on his paws. I think he was trying to tell Mom he would never, ever do it again.

I don't think she believed him though.

☺livia

Big Mess Thursday

You'll never believe what happened at school today.

Matilda and I were working quietly on our nature projects in class when we heard a loud **BANG!** And then a **Crash!**

And then some munching, crunching sounds, right outside our classroom.

And guess what we saw when we looked out the window?

The back half of a dog, sticking out of a trash can.

This is what we said next. (Very softly, so our teacher, Mr. Platt, couldn't hear us.)

Matilda: That dog looks like Bob.
Me: No it doesn't.
Matilda: Yes it does. It's got the same legs. And the same feet. And the same color hair.

Me: It can't be Bob.

Matilda: Why not?

Me: Bob's at home in our backyard.

Matilda: Are you sure?

Me: One hundred percent sure. He's probably digging a hole right now so he can bury Dad's slippers again.

Then the front half of the dog came out of the trash can backward. And guess what?

It was Bob!

He must have **smelled** the trash all the way from our place!

Matilda poked my arm and said,

I didn't want to get Bob into trouble. But I didn't want him wandering around the streets getting into **more** trouble either.

So I put my hand up and said, "Mr. Platt? My dog's outside our classroom. And he's raiding the trash cans. And making a big mess." And then I pointed out the window.

Everyone in my class rushed over to the window so they could see Bob too!

It took Mr. Platt a long time to get them all back in their seats again.

Mr. Platt told Matilda and me to catch Bob and take him to the office before he made more mess on the playground. And to ask Mrs. Gupta (the office lady) to call Mom.

Mom had to come all the way to school to get him.

She wasn't very happy about that. 🙁

🙂livia

PS This is a map that shows how Bob escaped. See? I told you Bob loves digging holes. Now we know he's good at jumping fences too. 🙂

Ninja Friday

Mom and I took Bob to the vet for a checkup after school. The vet checked his ears and his eyes and his heartbeat. Mom told the vet all about Bob and the trash cans. And digging holes under our fence.

And guess what the vet said? Bob might be doing **naughty things** that get him into trouble because he is **very bouncy** and **full of energy**.

She says we need to find him something to do to help him use all that **bouncy energy up!**

So when I got home I wrote some **Energy-Using-Up ideas** for Bob to try in my special Planning Book.

IDEA (1). Join our soccer team!

PROBLEM: He might run away with the ball. Then eat it. ☹

IDEA 2. Go roller-skating with me!

PROBLEM: He might fall off. Or crash into a tree. Or one of our neighbors. ☹

IDEA 3. Collect our newspaper from the front yard and bring it inside!

Newspaper

PROBLEM: He might collect all our neighbors' newspapers as well. ☹

Newspapers

I was just thinking up another **Energy-Using-Up idea** when I heard laughing. And squealing. And more laughing. And it was coming from outside. So I looked out my window and guess what I saw?

Matilda and her little brothers, Benny and Ollie. They were jumping around in their **playhouse** next door.

So I ran downstairs and out into the backyard. Then I called out to Matilda through the hole in our back fence.

Matilda: Hi, Olivia!

Me: What are you doing?

Matilda: Jumping. And swinging. And climbing.

Me: Why?

Matilda: Ollie and Benny and I are playing Ninja Knights. We made our own obstacle course in the playhouse.

Me: Awesome!

Matilda: What are you doing?

Me: Trying to find ways to use up Bob's energy, so he won't get into trouble all the time.

Matilda: Bring him over here! He can be a Ninja Knight too!

YES! BRILLIANT!

IDEA 4. We could all play Ninja Knights together!

Except . . .

PROBLEM: Bob is too big and bouncy to jump around in a playhouse. He might break something. Or hurt himself.

Thinking of ways to use up Bob's energy is really hard. There are TOO MANY PROBLEMS!

And then . . .

I had the best idea yet.

Matilda and I could make our own Ninja Dog-Knight course, just for Bob. With lots of special parts for bouncy dogs.

So I told Matilda I'd come back to play with them tomorrow. Then I went straight up to my room to design the plans for the Dog-Knight course.

It is going to be perfect!

☺livia

Super Saturday

Here is the Ninja Dog-Knight course we made in my backyard! It took us **all day**.

Mom helped Matilda and me to make it. We used lots of stuff we found around the house and in our shed. Like ladders and flowerpots and old planks of wood.

First we walked Bob around his new course on a leash. He loved weaving through the soccer cones the best. He didn't even try to steal any of them!

He was a bit scared of the dark tunnel we made. So Max got down on his hands and knees and crawled through it first, to show him what to do. And then I put a big dog biscuit at the end of it. Bob raced through the tunnel and gobbled it all up. ☺

We used more dog treats to train him to jump through the hula-hoop. Now he's a **star hula-hoop jumper!**

For his final trick, Bob had to rescue his favorite **squeaky toy** from Max's old wading pool.

Bob ran and crawled and jumped his way around the course six times!

He loves it!

I think he's going to sleep really well tonight. ☺

☺livia

Sunday Surprise

Something **very** exciting happened today!

We went to visit Great-nanna Peggy at Golden Gardens. Great-nanna Peggy is Dad's nanna. We call her GNP. ☺

GReat-
NANNA
Peggy
= G N P

(That's not the exciting thing though.)

Bob came to visit GNP too. GNP loves Bob.
And Bob loves GNP. She always gives him
lots of cuddles. Even when he's being a
little bit naughty. ☺

Golden Gardens is the name of the place
where GNP lives. Dad says it's called that
because it's full of Golden Oldies. Like
GNP's bestie, Pearl.

Pearl wears lots of sparkly jewelry, and flowers in her hair. Mom says she's traveled to every country in the world. Pearl tells the best stories! And she can burp the whole alphabet! I can only get up to E.

And there's Harry, who lives in the room around the corner from GNP. He's always **whistling** and **singing happy tunes.** Harry is a very good dancer. He showed me how to do a dance that all the Golden Oldies know called the fox-trot.

Sometimes we dance together at Golden Hour, when all the Oldies get together to eat snacks and have fun.

Harry

ME

Ella says GNP's home is called Golden Gardens because the garden beds are full of gold nuggets and coins!

But they're not. I checked. ☹

Sometimes Ella thinks she's SO smart, just because she's older than me.

One day I'm going to invent an invisible box and put Ella inside it. Then she'll know who the smart one **really** is. Hehehe. ☺

It's Great-nanna Peggy's 90th birthday today. We took her a birthday cake and **heaps** of **presents**.

(That's not the **very exciting thing** either. I'll tell you all about it soon!)

I gave GNP one of the science experiments I've been working on up in my room. I've been finding out all about how to grow MOLD.

First of all I dipped different types of food in water. Then I put them inside glass jars.

GRAPES

CHEESE

BREAD

BLUEBERRY muffin

SLICES of Lemon

I waited for a few days.
Not much happened
on the first day.

Or the second day.

Or the third day.

But on the **fourth** day, guess what
happened?

All the different
things started to
grow lovely moldy
mold! ☺ ☺

The jar with the cheese in it turned
out the best! It looks **really pretty!**
So I gave GNP that one to keep on the
windowsill in her room.

We were all just about to sing the Happy Birthday song when Max said,

Hey, where's BOB?

Oh no! We'd lost Bob!

Oops!

←--Max

I have to stop writing now. Dad just called me for dinner. I'll tell you all about what happened next (and also the very exciting thing) when I come back!

☺livia

After Dinner

We frantically searched GNP's room, looking for Bob!

In the bathroom part.

Under her bed.

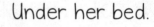

Inside her closet.

Behind the TV set.

But Bob had **completely vanished**.

Dad asked Ella and me to look for him in the hallways around GNP's room. Then he and Max went outside to look for him in the garden.

GNP waved goodbye to us.

I hope you find him, girls.

So did we!

The hallway was **very loooooong**. It was a little bit like the **Tunnel of Doom** in Bob's Ninja Dog-Knight course. There were lots of doors along it that all looked **exactly the same.**

Ella and I had a **big argument** about which way to go to look for Bob.

"Let's go this way," Ella said, pointing left.

"But he probably went **that** way," I said, pointing right.

"**This** way," said Ella.

"No, **that** way."

"THIS WAY!"

"THAT WAY!"

Mrs. Marsh is the lady who runs Golden Gardens. She has a big office that you have to walk past when you come in the front doors. And she owns a bird called Sweet Pea.

Sweet Pea can **talk!** All the Golden Oldies love him. Especially Pearl and GNP.

Mrs. Marsh walks around the building with a big clipboard, looking important. She **shushes** us if we get too noisy when we come to visit GNP. Or tells us not to run in the hallways.

Running in the hallways is Max's and my favorite thing to do at Golden Gardens. We are always getting into big trouble with Mrs. Marsh for doing it. ☹

NOOo RUNNING!!

WHEEEEE!

And guess what happened next?

Mrs. Marsh **did** hear us! She came **marching** right up to where we were standing outside GNP's door. Sweet Pea was sitting on her shoulder.

"SSSHHHH!"

Mrs. Marsh told us. "Some of the residents are having their afternoon naps."

Oops!

Ella and I looked at each other.

Sorry, Mrs. Marsh.

Then we crept off down the long, spooky hallway on our tiptoes, looking for Bob. We kept walking. And turning corners. And walking some more. It was like being inside a giant zigzaggy maze.

And then suddenly we heard some tinkly music. And people singing. And a howling sound.

We ran down to the end of the hallway and into a big lounge room. And guess what?

It was Bob!

He was sitting next to a piano with lots of Golden Oldies around him. Harry and Pearl were there too!

Everyone was singing along with the music. Bob was singing the loudest!

I waited until the music finished and everyone stopped singing. Then I said, "Come on, Bob. It's time to go home now."

But all the Golden Oldies wanted Bob to stay.

They kept giving him lots of cuddles and pats.

I could tell Bob wanted to stay too. He loves getting cuddles and pats. And someone even gave him a yummy cookie from the cookie jar!

And then . . .

Mrs. Marsh turned up. And she had her arms folded like she was really cranky.

Oops!

Here are the things I thought she was going to say:

But guess what? Mrs. Marsh didn't say any of those things!

She looked around at all the **big smiles** on the Golden Oldies' faces. And then she asked us if Bob would like to be a Golden Gardens Visiting Dog!

And if Ella and I would like to be Visiting-Dog Assistants!

And *that* was the **very exciting thing.** 😮

☺livia

A Bit Later

Guess what? Ella said she was going to be too busy rehearsing her dance for the school play to be a Visiting-Dog Assistant.

So I get to do it! AWESOME!

I can't wait to get started!

Mom and Dad said being a Visiting-Dog Assistant was too big a job for just one person though. And that I should ask a friend to help me.

So now Matilda will be
coming with me instead.

It's going to be
WICKED COOL!

Matilda

☺

First Visit Wednesday

Today was Bob's first visit to the Golden
Gardens Aged Care Home as a Visiting Dog.
Matilda and I took him after school.

Ella designed a **cute little outfit** for him, so everyone would know he wasn't just any old dog. He was the official Golden Gardens Visiting Dog!

GNP introduced him to all her friends so they would know his name.

Harry and Pearl already know him, of course.

Some of GNP's friends, like Dot and Lina, weren't in the lounge today, so we visited them in their rooms instead!

And then . . .

Something really bad happened.

We took Bob into the dining room for
afternoon tea.

And he jumped up
onto the table
and ate some of
the cakes.

Then he bounced against the tea cart and
the big china teapot fell off and smashed.

Oops!

Mrs. Marsh wasn't very happy. She said not to bring Bob back until he **learns some manners**.

☹livia

Matilda and I have been doing **special training** lessons with Bob all week.

We taught him to sit **nicely** and **quietly** when he's in a room full of people.

And not to jump up on anything. Even if he **really, really** wants to eat it!

We took Bob back to
Golden Gardens after
school today and
showed Mrs. Marsh
what a **good dog**
he was.

He was, too . . . until
he saw Mr. Kachinsky's
slippers. They were
sitting in the hallway,
outside Mr. Kachinsky's
room.

Bob **loves** slippers.

He loves licking them.

And chewing them.

But most of all,
he loves burying
them in the
backyard. Just
like he does with
Dad's.

And that is exactly
what he did.

Oops!

I don't think Mrs. Marsh was very happy about that either. ☹

Bob sang really nicely at Golden Hour though. ☺

☺livia

Splish Splash Saturday

Matilda and I took Bob back to Golden Gardens today.

We'd made him do his **Energy-Using-Up Ninja Dog-Knight** course a few times first, so he wasn't too **bouncy**. And we gave him his dinner early, so he wasn't too hungry.

Or **licky**. Or **chewy**.

Bob was being really good, sitting down nicely next to all the Golden Oldies so they could give him lots of **pats** and **cuddles**. Mrs. Vella even read him a story!

And then . . .

MRS. Vella

Flossy came along. Flossy is the Golden Gardens **Resident Cat**. She has her own **special** cat bed in the laundry room.

Flossy looked at Bob. And Bob looked at Flossy.

Then Bob decided to play a game, just like he does with Donkey.

He **chased Flossy** into the dining room,

round and round the kitchen,

and in and out of people's rooms.

Then he chased her out into the garden—
straight into the fishpond.

Oops.

Mrs. Marsh came running out of her
office. She picked up Flossy and wrapped
her in her stripy scarf.

And then she spoke the Words of Doom.

That was definitely Bob's last chance. Take him home, please. NOW!

And then we all walked sadly home.

☺livia

Sorry Sunday

Matilda and I went back to Golden Gardens today. Ella helped us to bake lots of cupcakes for the Golden Oldies, to make up for all the ones Bob ate last week.

We brought Bob with us, so he could say goodbye to everyone. He loved being a Visiting Dog. He's really going to miss all his new friends.

And then something else really bad happened. As soon as we arrived, he ran inside and disappeared.

Again!

Matilda and I ran **up and down all the hallways,** calling out his name.

We asked all GNP's friends if they'd seen him.

But nobody had. We couldn't find him anywhere. ☹

And then, suddenly, Bob came lolloping toward us!

I tried to get him to sit nicely and quietly, in case Mrs. Marsh saw him and told him off for running in the hallways.

But Bob wouldn't sit! He kept barking and pulling at my arm. Then he trotted off down the hallway.

Every now and then he'd stop and look back at us.

"He wants us to follow him!" I told Matilda.

Matilda and I ran up and down the twisty hallways, following Bob.

Past Pearl's room.

Past Lina's room.

Past GNP's room.

Until, finally, Bob stopped outside an open door. Then he barked again.

Matilda and I looked inside. And guess whose room it was?

Harry's!

Harry was on the floor. He didn't look too good. Bob ran in and sat quietly next to him.

Oh dear. I can't get up!

I told him, "Don't worry, Harry. We're here now!"

Lots of things happened next.

Mrs. Marsh came rushing in. And so did Sweet Pea!

Two strong nurses helped Harry to stand up. Then they made him nice and comfy in his armchair.

Harry

Everyone said Bob was a hero for helping Harry. Even Mrs. Marsh. She told us we could bring Bob to visit anytime we want!

I think Bob will like that. Though he's probably always going to be a little bit naughty. 😊

☺livia

OLiVia'S Secret Scribbles